To my daughters——Never forget that your true strength comes from an all-powerful Father
who loves you more than you could ever know —*glenn*

For my Grandpa Fred and Grandpa Dale, who have both served our country with honor —*brandon*

ALADDIN/Mercury Radio Arts, Inc.

An imprint of Simon & Schuster Children's Publishing Division

1230 Avenue of the Americas, New York, NY 10020

First Aladdin/Mercury Radio Arts hardcover edition October 2011

Text copyright © 2011 by Mercury Radio Arts, Inc.   Illustrations copyright © 2011 by Brandon Dorman

For information about special discounts for bulk purchases, please contact Simon & Schuster Special Sales at 1-866-506-1949 or business@simonandschuster.com.

The Simon & Schuster Speakers Bureau can bring authors to your live event. For more information or
to book an event contact the Simon & Schuster Speakers Bureau at 1-866-248-3049 or visit our website at www.simonspeakers.com.

Designed by Karin Paprocki

The text of this book was set in Wade Sans Light.   The illustrations for this book were rendered digitally.

Manufactured in the United States 0911 PCR

2 4 6 8 10 9 7 5 3 1

Library of Congress Cataloging-in-Publication Data

Schoebinger, Chris.

The snow angel / illustrated by Brandon Dorman ; adapted by Chris Schoebinger ; original story by Glenn Beck. —— 1st Aladdin hardcover ed. p. cm.

Summary: With their parents struggling to make ends meet, Anna and Lily grow tired of always eating macaroni and cheese for supper and having their
Nana stay with them, but when Nana hears their complaints she tells a story about the magic that snow angels can bring.

[1. Family problems—Fiction. 2. Grandmothers—Fiction. 3. Hope—Fiction.] I. Dorman, Brandon, ill. II. Beck, Glenn. III. Title.

PZ7.D727596Sno 2011 [E]—dc23 2011025399

ISBN 978-1-4424-4448-5   ISBN 978-1-4424-4455-3 (eBook)

The Snow Angel
A PICTURE BOOK

Illustrated by
Brandon Dorman

Adapted by
Chris Schoebinger

Original story by
GLENN BECK
with NICOLE BAART

ALADDIN/MERCURY RADIO ARTS, INC.
New York London Toronto Sydney New Delhi

THE MACARONI and cheese was never very good when Dad made it. But with Mom picking up a job at the grocery store at night, Dad's mac and cheese was becoming a regular occurrence.

"Can't we have something else tonight?" Ryan asked. But his father wasn't paying attention; his eyes were glued to the old television set in the living room.

The news was on and the announcer was speaking in a very serious tone. ". . . and that means millions of Americans cannot find jobs. Meanwhile, in the Middle East, the war continues for its ninth straight year. . . ."

"DAD!" Ryan yelled, trying to get his attention. "Lily and I are tired of macaroni and cheese. Can't we have something else?"

"No, we can't," his father replied. "Like I told you last night and the night before, I don't want to hear any more questions about dinner. Now eat fast and go get ready for bed, I'm late for work and Grandma will be here soon."

Grandma. Again. Ryan and Lily loved their grandma, but enough was enough—she'd been over the last five nights in a row to watch them.

"Why?" Lily whined. "We don't want Grandma to come over again. We don't want this macaroni and cheese again. And we don't want you and Mom to leave again. Why can't you just stay home with us like you used to?"

"Lily, I'm sorry, but we can't do that." He put his dish into the sink as they walked out of the room, dejected.

Grandma listened quietly to the whole conversation from the living room——no one knew she was there.

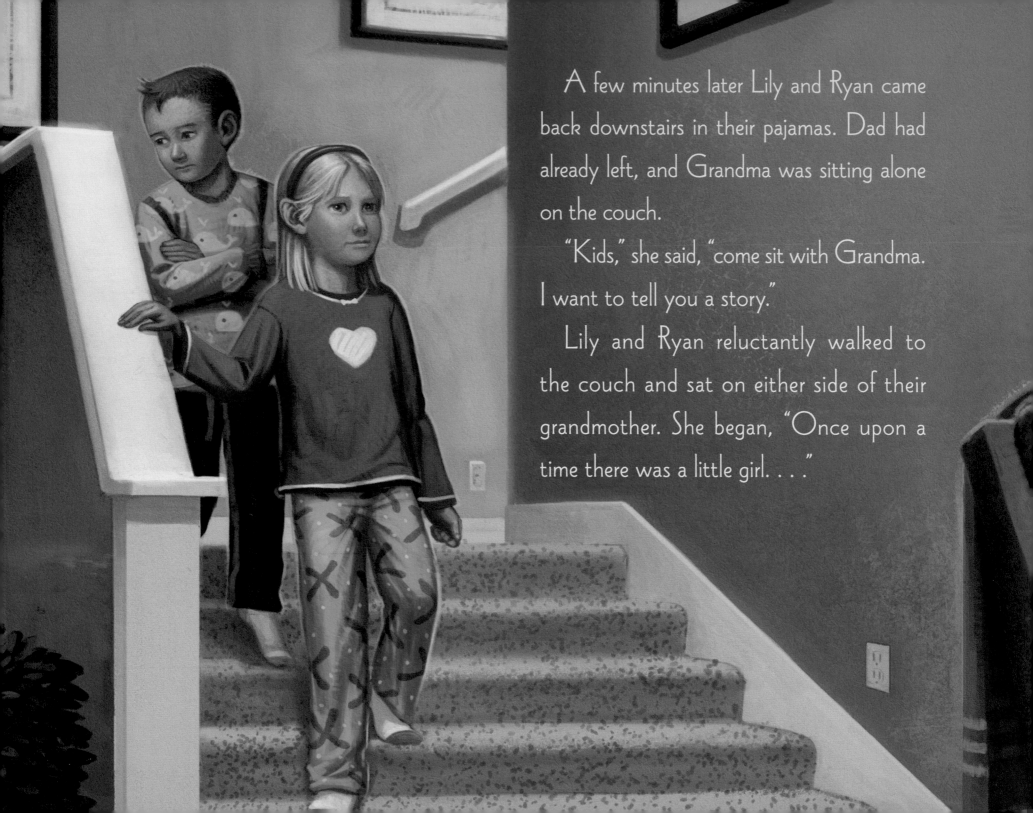

A few minutes later Lily and Ryan came back downstairs in their pajamas. Dad had already left, and Grandma was sitting alone on the couch.

"Kids," she said, "come sit with Grandma. I want to tell you a story."

Lily and Ryan reluctantly walked to the couch and sat on either side of their grandmother. She began, "Once upon a time there was a little girl. . . ."

As if on cue the children chimed in, "Was she a princess? Did she live in a castle? Was she eaten by a dragon?"

"Patience, children. Patience," Grandma said. "This is not a fairy tale. In fact, it's much, much better——because it's real."

"This little girl happened to live during a time when things in America were very difficult. Soldiers were fighting in other countries, jobs were hard to find, and most nights dinner was whatever vegetables she could find in the garden.

"The girl's mother worked hard all day and night to make uniforms for the army——and her father was one of the brave soldiers who went over to Europe to protect us. They were both gone a lot and the little girl missed them very much.

"One day the girl's father came home for a short break. The two of them played together every day from morning to night. On the day her daddy had to go back to Europe, it started to snow for the first time all winter. He took the little girl outside and showed her how to make snow angels on the front lawn.

"The father explained to his daughter that snow angels are magical, because if you make one for someone you love, it stores all of that love right in their heart. The angels, he told her, would always be with her, even when he couldn't be.

"And he was right! Even after he went back to the war, the little girl never felt alone again. His snow angel was always there with her."

When the story was done Lily's face slowly began to brighten. "Grandma," she asked, "were you the little girl in that story? Was it your daddy who showed you how to make snow angels?"

"Yes, it was me," Grandma replied. "And I never forgot that day."

Grandma continued, "I know you miss your parents when they're at work. And I know that you don't want to eat the same thing for dinner every night, but it's all because your mom and dad love you so much and want to protect you. Now that we all know about the magic of snow angels, we can show your parents that you love and remember them, even when they're working so hard.

"Sometimes they work so hard that they forget about the magic of snow angels. And that's where you two can help."

"But, Grandma," Ryan replied, "there's no snow."

Grandma just smiled and said, "I think I have an idea."

The next morning Lily and Ryan woke up early and met downstairs. Twenty minutes later, they walked into their parents' bedroom with two plates.

"We made you breakfast in bed," Lily said proudly.

Mom and Dad were stunned; they'd never had breakfast in bed before. Especially not macaroni and cheese.

"We couldn't use the stove," Ryan said, "so we just skipped that part of the instructions."

Dad took a big spoonful of the crunchy macaroni and smiled. "It's the best macaroni and cheese I've ever had."

When breakfast was done, Mom and Dad followed the kids downstairs. At the bottom they stopped suddenly and gasped. Hundreds of paper snow angels had been strung together and hung from the ceiling. It was a virtual winter wonderland.

"Grandma said that snow angels are magic," Lily said softly. "And we wanted to give some of that magic to you."

Mom and Dad looked on in wonder at the gift they'd been given. Mom tried to speak but her eyes began to water. "Thank you. . . . Thank you so much."

Who do you know that needs some magic?
Make them a snow angel and share your love.

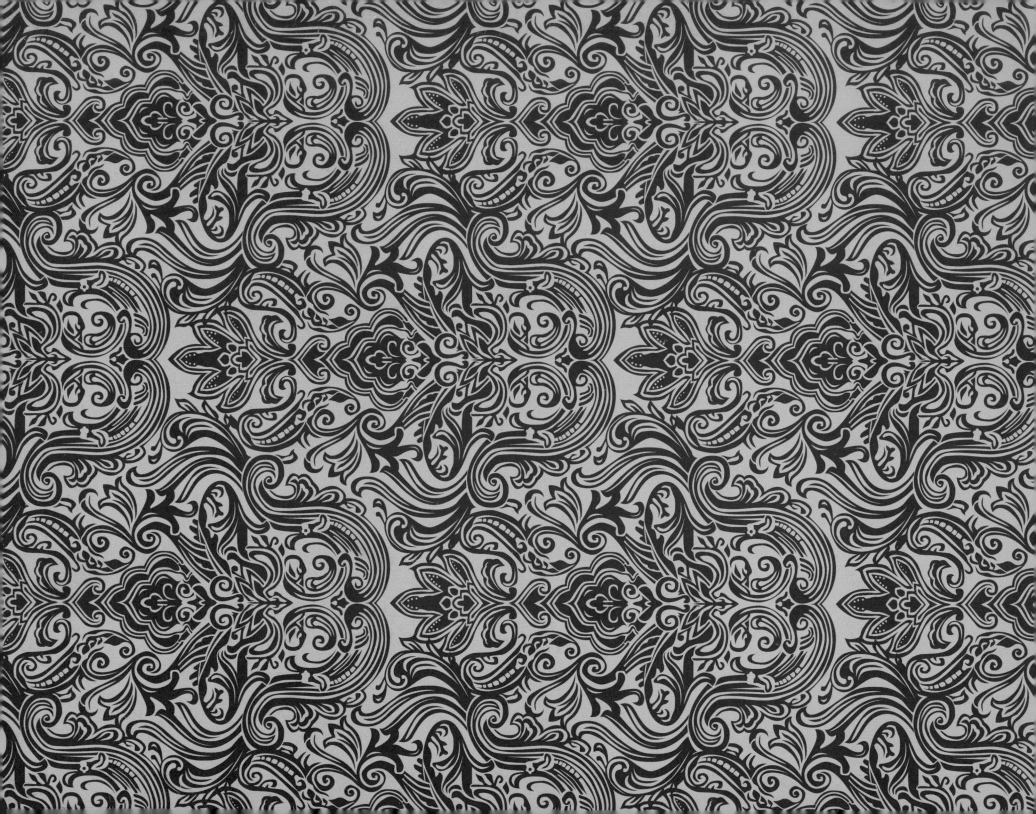